D0463484

Put Beginning Readers on the Right Track with
ALL ABOARD READING™

The All Aboard Reading series is especially for beginning readers. Written by noted authors and illustrated in full color, these are books that children really and truly *want* to read—books to excite their imagination, tickle their funny bone, expand their interests, and support their feelings. With four different reading levels, All Aboard Reading lets you choose which books are most appropriate for your children and their growing abilities.

Picture Readers—for Ages 3 to 6
Picture Readers have super-simple texts, with many nouns appearing as rebus pictures. At the end of each book are 24 flash cards—on one side is the rebus picture; on the other side is the written-out word.

Level 1—for Preschool through First-Grade Children
Level 1 books have very few lines per page, very large type, easy words, lots of repetition, and pictures with visual "cues" to help children figure out the words on the page.

Level 2—for First-Grade to Third-Grade Children
Level 2 books are printed in slightly smaller type than Level 1 books. The stories are more complex, but there is still lots of repetition in the text, and many pictures. The sentences are quite simple and are broken up into short lines to make reading easier.

Level 3—for Second-Grade through Third-Grade Children
Level 3 books have considerably longer texts, harder words, and more complicated sentences.

All Aboard for happy reading!

To Jeff, with love always —G.H.

For my good friends,
Vita and Jim Rhodes —J.S.

Text copyright © 1993 by Gail Herman. Illustrations copyright © 1993 by Jerry Smath. All rights reserved. Published by Grosset & Dunlap, Inc., a member of Penguin Putnam Books for Young Readers, New York. ALL ABOARD READING is a trademark of The Putnam & Grosset Group. GROSSET & DUNLAP is a trademark of Grosset & Dunlap, Inc. Published simultaneously in Canada. Printed in the U.S.A.

Library of Congress Cataloging-in-Publication Data. Herman, Gail, 1959–   Double-header / by Gail Herman ; illustrated by Jerry Smath.   p.   cm. — (All aboard reading)   "Level 1, preschool-grade 1."   Summary: Bob and Rob Headley, a two-headed monster, love doing everything together, especially playing catcher on a team in the Little Monster League. [1. Monsters—Fiction. 2. Baseball—Fiction.] I. Smath, Jerry, ill. II. Title. III. Series. PZ7.H4513Do 1993   [E]—dc20   92-34175   CIP   AC

ISBN 0-448-40157-6   J

ALL
ABOARD
READING™

Level 1
Preschool–Grade 1

DOUBLE-HEADER

By Gail Herman
Illustrated by Jerry Smath

Grosset & Dunlap • New York

Hello. Hello.

We are the Headleys.

I am Bob, says Bob.

I am Rob, says Rob.

We do everything together.

We have to.

We are stuck with each other.

And that is just fine.

We like having two heads.
It is better than one.
We can sing duets.
We can look both ways
when we cross the street.

We always agree.
We hate vegetables
and wearing ties.

We like

peanut butter and jelly,

scary movies, and baseball.

We love to play baseball.

Today we play
the Frankees.

Can you guess our position?

It is catcher.

We keep two eyes on the ball

and two eyes on the bases.

We are good players.

Play ball!

We catch.

We hit.

We run around the bases.

The Frankees are good.

But we win the first game.

Hooray!

The Frankees are mad.

You will not beat us again,

they say.

But we know we will win.
Why? Today we are playing
a doubleheader!
Ha, says Bob.
Ha, says Rob.

The second game starts.

It is very close.

We are behind

by one run.

FRANKEES 9
MONSTERS 8

Now it is
the last inning.
There are two outs.
And we are up at bat.

Our team needs two runs.

We have two heads.

We can score two runs.

It is in the rule book.

18

Here is the pitch.

Our four eyes watch the ball.

We swing.

Crack!

The ball flies.

We run to first base.

We are safe.

We run to second base.

Safe.

Third base.

Safe.

We start to run home.

Uh-oh.

One of the Frankees
has the ball.

She is coming closer.

We look right.

We are halfway home.

We look left.

We are halfway to third.

Which way should we run?

Home! shouts Bob.

Third! shouts Rob.

Home!

Third!

We run both ways at once.

We do not get anywhere.

Uh-oh.

Here comes the Frankee.

We run faster.

But still

we do not get anywhere.

She tags us.

We are out.

We have lost the game.

Your fault, says Bob.

Your fault, says Rob.

The game is over.

But we stay put.

We wait for the other one

to say I am sorry.

It gets dark and cold.

But we do not move.

Plink. Plink.

It begins to rain.

But still we do not move.

Then we remember.
It is Fright Night
at the movies.
They are showing
HUMAN BEINGS
and
HUMAN BEINGS 2.

Ah! we scream.

A double feature!

We look at each other.

We smile.

HUMAN BEINGS 2
(THE PICNIC)

Let's head to the
movie theater, we say.
Ha, says Bob.
Ha, says Rob.

There is nothing like a
scary double feature
to bring us together.

Friends? says Bob.

Friends! says Rob.

We always agree.

Well, almost always.